Love & DRILL

A 6ix story

TYLER GORDON

Tellwell Talent
www.tellwell.ca

ISBN
978-0-2288-3888-3 (Paperback)
978-0-2288-3889-0 (eBook)

Prologue

"You hear that, Zee?" Max, barely three years of age, questions with extreme anxiety. But his brother Zeke lays in bed and doesn't wake up. Scared for his life, Max has a gut feeling that something is wrong and it isn't just another movie he hears from their living room. Crawling out of bed, Max gets on his hands and knees to be as quiet as possible on his way to the door. Max opens the door slowly… just about an inch so that he can investigate without being seen.

To Max's surprise, he sees a man standing over his naked father with a riot shotgun in his hands that reads "*Rizzo*" in cursive engraved along the bottom of the drum attachment.

He hears the mumbling of his father and the man conversing, but he can't make out any of what they are saying. He is shocked at this never-before-experienced scene of danger... Max is paralyzed with fear.

Gunshot

Chapter 1

Introduction

August 2004

Zeke and Max Fitzner, inseparable brothers with only four years' age difference, arrive at their grandmother Miriam's apartment building.

Max scoots over and follows Zeke out of the back seat of their grandmother's black 2001 sedan. "Grama, how long do we have to stay with you until Mom comes to pick us up?" Zeke asks his grandmother while adjusting his red and blue superhero backpack.

Some heavy sighs escape Miriam's throat. The last couple of months have been the most emotionally draining she has ever been through.

Her daughter-in-law has been missing for almost two months now, and — unrelated or not — a month later her only son was murdered over a drug dispute. She knows she is Max and Zeke's sole provider now. No time to grieve; she bears the responsibility of raising these boys to be responsible for their actions and to not end up in the same situation as their father.

After entering their grandmother's apartment — Number 1208 — Max and Zeke are shown their new room where they will now be staying. The room is about the same size that they were used to at their parents' house. Two single beds are separated by a ceiling-to-floor window and bordered by nightstands against the wall. Max throws down his suitcase and jumps into bed.

Zeke walks toward his bed and sits down, facing Max.

"Yo Max, I know you don't know this, but I really don't think Mom is coming back."

Max starts skinning his teeth. "The police say they're still looking for evidence, though," Max pleads to his brother.

"Yeah, but they're just telling us that to give us hope... I know Dad was a dangerous guy out here in these streets and I think you should know Mom was involved too. I think that's why they always used to leave us at Grama's every weekend," Zeke says while getting up and sitting beside his brother on his bed.

Placing a hand on little Max's shoulder, Zeke continues, "But never mind that. Listen, Max... **WE** *are all we have. Now... to the end.* I'm gonna stop playing basketball so much so I can look out for you and make sure you're safe until I take my last breath. I promise you that as your older brother. And anyone who messes with our family will get what's coming to them one way or another." Zeke knows that Max might not fully understand the circumstances; all he will understand is that his parents aren't coming back into his life.

Zeke, returning to his bed, starts to think about how he will have to adjust to this new life. Now that his father and mother are gone, he feels as if he is the sole protector of his younger brother. The lessons that his father had ingrained in him at an early age will help guide him to be the man that he thinks his father wanted him to be.

"Come eat," shouts Miriam from the dining room as she places two bowls of macaroni and cheese on the dining room table.

As they are nearing the end of their meal, their grandmother returns and has a seat with them at the table...

"Listen, Zeke and Max, things are going to be a little different than what you're used to," Miriam says in a calming voice. She can tell that Zeke may already be starting to understand what's going on with the family, but she decides to explain their new living situation to them both at the same time.

Miriam extends one arm each to the children with her palms facing up, and she says, "You boys will be living with me from now on. I will be taking care of you now. When you leave school, you take the bus and come here after. If you need something, I'll buy it for you."

Knocks at the door

"Hold on," Miriam says as she gets up from the table to answer the door. From Zeke's perspective, he can see the door behind Max's chair.

"Hello, Mrs. Fitzner, I am Officer Noah, and this is my recruit, Gregory, and we're just here to do a check and make sure everything is going okay with the relocation."

"Yes, Officer, we're doing just fine. We're actually just having dinner at the moment."

Max -	3	Max Fitzner
Zeke -	7	Zeke Fitzner
Grama -	52	Miriam Fitzner
Officer Noah -	31	Noah Gerald
Recruit Gregory -	23	Gregory Andrews

Chapter 2

First day of school

Fall 2008

Four years have passed since the night Max's father was murdered. At Southlee Public School, where Max and Zeke Fitzner are enrolled, Max is walking to his second-grade class with his head held high, sporting his new style of cornrows that just reach the bottom of his neck. Barely holding the straps of his book bag draped over his shoulders, Max walks to his desk. He sits in the fifth row of the leftmost column.

As Max is releasing the straps of his bag to sit down, another student approaches him; it's

Jameel. "Yo Max, you have those chewy candies from the store where everything is a dollar? I got a quarter for you."

"I gotchu, Jams," Max responds while reaching in his bag.

Jameel is a muscular child with a short-tapered fade. He is often feared by other children who won't spend the time to actually talk to him.

They make the exchange. Max isn't the type of student who gets 100% on his tests and quizzes. Homework, quizzes, and tests aren't things that interest him; what matters to Max is making money. He learned at a very young age from being around his father that money brings power.

"Yo, what're you sayin after school?" Jams asks Max.

"I'm 'bout to go to the store again after school, get some more supplies," Max answers as he points to the rest of the candies and gum packs in his bag. Jams and Max are school friends but they've never hung out outside of school. "You tryna come with me and get some stuff; I just got the newest basketball game and

I can whoop you in that after," Max offers Jameel.

"Yea, cool, I'm there, and yea right, you could never!" Jams says while laughing.

"I already body you in real life on the court, so in the game it's gone be the same thing," Jams adds.

"Yeaaaa, okay, we'll see. Bet your share of what we get from the store after school then."

"Hahaha, it's a Jams says.

"Max and Jameel, why are you boys talking during reading time? Open up your books. You know the first 20 minutes of class are for reading," Mrs. Crocker says from behind her desk at the front of the class.

After making sure his brother gets to his class, Zeke runs down the hallway toward his own class. Running carefully, Zeke is trying to protect his new shoes from creasing. He makes it just on time. Ms. Johnson is waiting at the class door, ready to close it and send any latecomers for a late slip.

Max -	7	Max Fitzner
Zeke -	11	Zeke Fitzner
Jams -	7	Jameel Magou
Mrs. Crocker -	31	Jessica Crocker
Ms. Johnson -	40	Fiona Johnson

Chapter 3

New kids on the block

Summer 2006

Von and Andre Lampton's uncle, who is their guardian, is one of the most respected street bosses in Canada. He has had to flee the country for a while because of a situation that was getting too dangerous.

Trusting Andre, he makes the two brothers move to East York of Toronto. Dre is free to do whatever he wants granted he ensures Von will remain in school and graduate high school.

Andre, being a *protégé* hustler after his uncle, is able to find a two-bedroom apartment that suits the needs of him and his little brother.

Von is a big fan of movies like *Juice*, *Paid in Full*, and *Belly*. He believes in loyalty until the end; that's the way his older brother Andre raises him.

Von doesn't have many people in his life, so he holds the ones he has dear. Von has never met his father because he was in jail at his birth; and he has no memories of his mother because she was murdered for infidelity while his father was doing time when he was three years old.

The only consistent person in his life is his cousin Andre.

This isn't the first time Andre has to take care of his little cousin, but this is the first time he has to move away from home. Dre figures that whoever his uncle has a problem with are some treacherous people if they're at war with HIM, so it's probably best not try to reach out to him until he reaches out to them. And to be on the safe side Andre figures it is best if they continue living as if they are cousins so that no history or past enemies could connect them.

Von - 9	Von Lampton
Dre - 20	Andre Lampton

Chapter 4

School Fight

February 2009

Jameel walks to the seating area of the cafeteria with his lunch tray carrying a slice of pizza, a big cookie, and chocolate milk. He sees Max sitting with three other people, so he joins the table.

"Yeo, what's good," Jameel says acknowledging the whole table. Max stops, his pizza just at his lips, when he notices Jameel.

"Ayee, whaddup Jams... This is Fitz and Marcus."

"What's good, Fitz n Marcus," Jams says while fixing his legs over the lunch bench. Fitz extends his hand to Jams for a handshake.

After, Marcus reaches over to Jameel for a handshake, but his handshake is aggressive — almost as to test him of strength or toughness. Jameel not only is the type to never back down, but if he even smelled a challenge, he would jump all over it.

Noticing the aggression of the handshake, Jameel immediately turns to face Marcus and squeezes his hand in return. Marcus pulls his hand while still interlocked with Jameel's so that he will be pulled over the lunch table.

In the same motion that Jameel is going forward, he uses it to push Marcus off the bench. Mindless of the age and size difference, Jams isn't going to be intimidated by anyone.

Fully mounted on top of Marcus, he pounds away at Marcus' guard, sneaking in a few hits to his forehead and chest. Max lifts his tray off the table so that his food won't get tossed on the ground. "Yeo, beat his ass, Jams," Max cheers on.

Walking with his tray down the aisle, Von notices the brawl going on at the back of the cafeteria. He can only recognize one person who is in his class: Fitz. Von runs over as the fight is over just in time to see the teacher on lunch supervision rushing through the door to grab the students.

Von notices Jams making a run out the opposite exit, and then he consciously drops his tray on the ground in the path of the teacher in hopes Jams can make his escape.

Fitz is shocked that a classmate he barely knows would risk getting in trouble for a stranger. The teacher steps and slips on the tray but doesn't fall to the ground...

Outside the principal's office sit Marcus, Max, Fitz, Von, and Jameel in a row.

Door opens

Mr. Psyfocks, standing at a sloppy, fat 5'8" wearing a cheap vomit-coloured plaid suit, says, "Von Lampton, come in first," while waving his hand into his office with an agitated look on his face. Marcus sniffles as he holds an ice pack to the left side of his forehead; Von stands up and walks calmly into the office.

They all get called one at a time to Mr. Psyfocks' office where they are asked to explain what transpired at lunch.

Jameel is the fourth person called into the office after Max, Jameel, and Fitz; he walks in and takes a seat on the chair directly in front of the principal's desk.

"So, Jameel, care to explain your side of what happened at yesterday's lunch?" Mr. Psyfocks interrogates Jameel.

Jameel knows that the only people who saw the whole event transpire were himself and the other four just outside the office. He is only close to Max, so he can't trust that the others won't tell on him. Being familiar with mischief, he knows that if they knew everything, they wouldn't be so vague with the questions they're asking. AHA! The lunch lady came in late, so they don't know what happened…

"I don't even know why I'm here," Jameel says with a straight face.

"Listen, boy… I've had enough of this nonsense. If none of you boys cooperate, things are going to be worse for you," Mr. Psyfocks says in a very stern voice.

Jameel remains silent.

"Do you know I could make it very hard for you to go to any school in this district if you're going to be causing this kind of trouble and fighting in this school?" Mr. Psyfocks declares.

Jameel remains silent.

"Okay, fine; I'll find out one way or another... You can go now," Mr. Psyfocks suggests.

Jameel gets up and leaves. Mr. Psyfocks follows behind him to the door and calls for the last student, Marcus Simpson.

Jams -	8	Jameel Magou
Max -	7	Max Fitzner
Fitz -	11	Zeke Fitzner
Von -	11	Von Lampton
Marcus -	11	Marcus Simpson
Mr. Psyfocks -	45	Anthony Psyfocks

Chapter 5

Detention

Valentine's Day 2009

Max, Jams, Fitz, and Von walk into room 109 and take seats together at the back of the class.

Chalk marks on the board

Mrs. Baxter underlines <u>DETENTION.</u>

"Listen, I don't want to hear anybody talking for the next hour," declares Mrs. Baxter as she pulls out her phone at the teacher's desk at the front of the classroom.

"That's fucked up; not gonna lie..." Max claims.

"What?" Fitz responds.

"Marcus isn't even here," Jams reveals. The four take looks around the class and there is only one other student in the classroom: a tall brown-skinned girl with long box braids sitting just a few seats in front of them.

"No, the fact that me and Zeke are here and we weren't even involved," Max retorts.

"Sounds like the Marcus boy told on y'all if he's the only one not here," Cinnamon explains while letting out a chuckle. "I saw what happened," she adds while turning to Von.

Jams isn't sure if he can trust Fitz or Von, but he remembers that Mr. Psyfocks said no one cooperated before him, and only Marcus was behind him.

"Fuck Marcus, yo," Jams voices.

"Yea, Marcus was a lame-ass, anyways," Fitz adds.

"Well, I just didn't want to see a man get caught," Von states.

"I rate you for that, fam... you're a real one," Jams responds to Von.

"That's nothin'. Don't worry about it; we only here for an hour," Von answers lightheartedly.

"Jams, I didn't think you was gone do all that to Marcus," Max says, laughing to the group.

"Fam, you know he was trying to son me," Jams says, laughing and rolling his eyes.

"Lucky he didn't try ME like that; I woulda had to end him," Max states jokingly.

At the end of the hour, the hand-twisted alarm clock rings. The four boys leave the building behind Cinnamon; they go left and she goes right.

"I'll catch y'all boys in a minute. Max, you good to make it home?" Zeke asks Max and turns the other way to run and catch up to Cinnamon to walk her home.

"Hey, wait up, Cinnamon," Zeke says, tapping her on the back. He hands her a rose that his grandmother had given him that morning. "Happy Valentine's Day."

"Wow, for meee!" Cinnamon exclaims as her heart melts. "What took you so long to give me something you had all day?" Cinnamon questions.

Caught off guard, Zeke reaches over his head to scratch it. "Well, I — wasn't sure if you already had one… I mean, look at you."

Cinnamon can't resist blushing while listening to Zeke, so she turns around and continues walking.

"Come on, you walking me home right? It's just this way," Cinnamon says to Zeke.

Fitz -	11	Zeke Fitzner
Max -	7	Maximus Fitzner
Jams -	7	Jameel Magou
Von -	11	Von Lampton
Cinnamon -	11	Cinnamon Lockheart
Mrs. Baxter -	26	Mikala Baxter

Chapter 6

An Eventful Day

March 2020

On a partially cloudy Friday afternoon, Max, Fitz, and Jams find themselves at the expensive watch store in Yorkdale Mall after Fitz has just upgraded his phone. Fitz is looking through the glass, caressing his chin while deciding which piece to get. Max and Jams are outside the store debating who is the best basketball player in the world.

In the middle of their debate, Max feels a shoulder brush his. "What the fuck, yo? Watch yourself," Max yells as he recovers and walks toward the man.

"Yea, ehh? Watch your girl, fam; she get her bundles from dead horses," the man says while doing a 360 and continuing on.

Fitz, hearing a commotion outside the store, rushes to the store exit to get a full grasp of what's going on. Just getting outside of the store he checks left... nothing. He checks right and sees Jams and Max kicking the stranger in the ribs.

Fitz runs over to both of them, yelling, "Yo, what the fuck goin' on Max; c'mon, we gotta get out of here."

After going back to Von's apartment, the guys decide they are going to smoke two Russian cream blunts of Lemon Haze. Max reaches in his black weed container that reads 'Get money' in gold writing, and he starts to roll.

It is about 8:30 p.m. The guys are in very high spirits laughing, joking, playing a basketball video game, and retelling the story from earlier from each point of view.

"You see how that nigga's tooth flew out," Jams says.

"Man, I ain't never waiting to get swung on; shit like that can happen," Von replies. "Yea, but Jams came rushing in with the swiftness; it was over before it started. Can't nobody fuck with us," Jams adds.

"Well, maybe if he was really as brave as he thought he was, he might've had a chance," Von says as if that were possible.

The guys are feeling on top of the world as if no one could possibly stand against them. After the blunts had burned out, Max beats Jams in the basketball video game three minutes into the fourth quarter in a match.

Fitz's phone rings. He takes a second to look at the number to see if he recognizes it; since he got a new phone, he lost his contacts.

"Yeeo Cinny?" Fitz answers, knowing it is his girlfriend Cinnamon.

"Oh yea, you got a new phone today. Yeah, it's me. Hey, baby, are you still coming to Mercedes' birthday tonight with me?"

"Oh, shit, that was tonight, huh? Where's it at again?" Fitz responds.

"We're seeing Lil Noseé live at Rebellion; you have to come through 'cause a bitch gon need some dick after the club."

Fitz chuckles and says, "Aii, I gotcho nasty ass," then hangs up.

"Yeo, mandem, I'm bout to head out stylll. Come to Rebellion tonight. It's my girlfriend's friend's birthday, so you already know all the girls in the city are gonna be there," Fitz says while standing up and putting his phone in his pocket.

"Ahliee yo, that's not a bad idea; stylll, I need to get like this fly guy and have the hoes flockin," Von says to Fitz.

They all agree to go to Rebellion for 11. Fitz and Max return to their house to shower and get ready. Fitz dresses in a brown and red plaid button up with black washed jeans that have a rip in the knee. Max puts on a brown varsity jacket over his white hoodie that reads "savage" in bright red writing across the chest with blue washed jeans and brown hiking boots.

Before leaving, Max puts on his white balaclava rolled up like a hat. "Yo, you coming with me, Zee, or you gonna drive yourself?" Max questions Zeke.

"Yeah, imma come with you and me and Cinny will get a cab back whenever."

"Bet."

Max drives his car — a black SUV — and brings his favourite gun; a .357 with a customized white handle with engravings on it, leaving it in the driver side door compartment for easy access. Max first heads back to Von's apartment to pick up Von and Jams to pull up to the club together.

After finding a parking spot three rows away from the entrance by a light pole, the guys know the bouncers so they walk through the side door at VIP. Fitz leads the guys inside because he has the best idea of who they're looking for.

"Found 'em," says Fitz as he taps Von behind him with his right hand and points with his left to the top tier where the celebration is going on.

"Man, this shit is extra packed tonight," Jams says while following behind Max.

The guys follow a bottle waitress over to the table where Cinnamon, Mercedes, and other ladies are seated.

"Hey baby," Fitz greets Cinnamon with a hug and a kiss. Cinnamon with her natural curly brown hair and long blue strapless dress, introduces her friends to Fitz's friends before they pour their first drink.

Max takes a quick interest in Cinnamon's friend Ashley. Standing 5 foot 8, she is the most beautiful brown-skinned woman Max has ever seen. She has side-swept bangs the colour of a rosewood ombre and lipstick to match.

Ashley taps Cinnamon on her arm and says, "Girll, who is that?? Beside Zeke... He is *fine*."

"I knew you'd want him. That's Zeke's little brother; he's just a year younger than you. He used to talk to Mercedes, but I think they're done. Ask her to introduce you," Cinnamon says to Ashley.

Max is exactly Ashley's type: rugged-looking with long box braid dreads that are split into four: two in front and two on his back. The first thing she notices is Max's height: he must have a full foot over her.

Mercedes and Ashley walk over to the booth where Max, Von, and Jams are sitting.

Max has a mysterious aura around him and she just has to find out more.

"You ladies enjoying your night?" Max says to Ashley and Mercedes as they approach the booth.

"Guess you ain't see us before, huh?" Mercedes responds to Max.

"Hello, Mercedes."

kisses teeth "Whatever. This is my friend Ashley; she's visiting from Montreal," Mercedes says to Max.

"I can introduce myself, Mercedes," Ashley says without taking her eyes off of Max.

Max chuckles and moves over in the booth to make room for Ashley. Seeing this, Mercedes walks off not in disbelief but in disdain.

Giving Max space to talk, Von and Jams head to the bar. Max admires Ashley's demeanour. She is a serious girl just like him. Wearing small round loop gold earrings and a thin gold necklace, she isn't doing too much, but she is still leagues above the other women in the club.

"You're a little early... I thought angels only came out on Sunday morning," Max says to Ashley, making her blush.

"Yeah, well, if I'm an angel, you a demon with that balaclava on your head."

"Well, maybe you can repent for my sins for me."

Max's beard is not fully grown-in and patchy. This feeds into his devilish-looking nature which is turning on Ashley even more.

Announcer: "Please Give it up for Lil Noseé, everyone."

At around 3:30 a.m., Fitz and Cinnamon have just gone home together after taking their birthday pictures with the one and only Sleight of Hand Flims, and Jams and Von are ready to leave. But Max is determined to find Ashley again before the night ends.

"Yo, just give me a second to find shorty then we out. I see the opposition in here, but he ain't nun I can't handle; y'all know me… Son of a gun," Max says to Von and Jam while gesturing a fist.

Jams and Von look at each other for confirmation and wait for Max to find his woman and head home. At this time, Jams and Von go to the bar to get one last drink as they wait. It takes Max no more than two minutes to find Ashley.

As Ashley is grabbing onto the hand of Max, who is leading them outside, Max messages the guys that he's on his way to the car and to meet him there so they can leave. Moments before placing his hand on the door to exit the club, their path is blocked. It is the same opp from Yorkdale.

"Nyah ehhhh, you thought shit was fucking sweet and we wouldn't catch you?" says the man.

Max stops dead in his tracks, surprisingly ecstatic. *"Don't let me get to my car,"* he whispers under his breath. "Y'all ain't on shit; fuck out my way," is what he actually says.

The second of the four opps that surround Max lifts his shirt to show the modified pistol in his waistband while styling a smirk right at Max. "I'll slap you with that on you, eh! Fawad outside," he says while pointing with his head toward the exit. Max takes the long way to exit the club to give him a few-second gap between him and the opps.

Max starts walking with Ashley toward his car, but then he whispers something in her ear, hugs her, and sends her away. There he sees Jams and Von waiting outside the car. "Ahhhh, she curved you, uhhh kid," Von says jokingly, but he quickly notices the serious expression on Max's face.

They know exactly what the look in Max's eyes is. Someone has messed with the wrong guy tonight.

Max remains silent, but he pulls his keys out of his pocket and unlocks the car to let them sit inside.

Jams sits behind the driver and Von is in the passenger seat. Max starts the car and rolls down his window and his balaclava, knowing the guys he just saw aren't going to give up looking for him so easily because of the incident at the mall. He does a loop of the parking lot, seemingly looking for them.

He spots them and lets out a short chuckle, filled with excitement. Max drives up to them and, without saying a word, he shoots the head off of the man that brandished the modified pistol.

The screams are so loud they can't be drowned out. The enemy gang turns around in complete and utter shock. Max drops the second man before any of them take their first step in running away.

"WHAT THE FUCKKKK!!!! WAIT, YO, WHO ARE THESE GUYSS???" questions Von.

"They just paged me on the way out here just now," Max states, surprisingly calm as he pulls the parking brake up and hangs half his body out the window, trying to aim and take a good shot at the last two opps running for their lives.

Max hits one of them in the top right of his shoulder blade; he falls over and starts crawling between the cars to get out of Max's sight. Max lets one more bullet ring out the nose of the .357 in an attempt to finish the victim he had already shot... He misses. "Damn," Max exhales loudly.

"DAMN! and I ain't even bring my strap," exclaims Jameel while violently shaking the headrest of Max in front of him. The vibrations of Jams' words hit the ears of Max and Von, and wheel screeches soon follow. They are skrrtin off.

"Yoo, that was some wild shit, bro; you really killed those niggas?" Jams exclaims as he leans forward through the opening of the front seats.

"Bro, what the fuck was that for; you're a fucking hot boy," says Von angrily, turning his head to face Max.

"Fuck em. Don't ever think you can run down on me and get away with it," Max says in a menacing tone.

Even though this is Max's first time taking lives he isn't remorseful. He is anxious that he might've been seen by someone in the distance, but he is satisfied to know they at least couldn't have seen his face.

Max -	19	Max Fitzner
Fit -	23	Zeke Fitzner
Cinnamon -	23	Cinnamon Lockheart
Jams -	19	Jameel Magou
Von -	23	Von Lampton
Ashley -	20	Ashley Gibson
Mercedes -	22	Mercedes Hawkin

Chapter 7

How do you like your eggs?

April 2020

Zeke, Max, and Miriam are having breakfast at the breakfast spot on College Street on a beautiful Sunday morning. Sitting at a table against the window, the three of them place their order.

Miriam orders an oatmeal bowl with blueberries, raspberries, and brown sugar, and an Earl Grey tea. Max orders triple chocolate banana pancakes with a strawberry banana smoothie.

Zeke, being the last one to make up his mind, places his order last. "Can I get uhh… French toast, eggs, and bacon please?" Zeke asks the waitress.

"No problem, sir; anything to drink?"

"Oh yea, lemme get, uh, hot chocolate."

"No problem. Your food is coming right up."

"So, Max, have you applied to college yet? I know you said you were going to take a year off of school to try and start your own business. Well, a year is up," Miriam interrogates Max. Zeke starts to laugh as his eyes widen from the blunt question.

"Grama, I'm doing fine with my business right now. I'll get around to it soon," Max replies in an attempt to end the conversation as quickly as possible.

"Listen, Max, I don't want you to grow old in this street life. There are only two ways out — death and jail — and with your luck, you might mix them," Miriam lectures.

"Don't worry about him, Grama. I watch his back just as much as my own," Zeke intervenes before answering a text from Cinnamon.

"And you, Zeke… these last couple weeks it looks like you've just been out of it. Is anything going on?" Miriam turns her attention to Zeke.

at Cinnamon's apartment

Locking her front door behind Mercedes, Cinnamon has a plastic drugstore bag in her right hand carrying only one item. She places the bag down on the island in the kitchen — which is the first room of the apartment — and takes out the pregnancy test.

"You sure you ready for this, girl?" Mercedes asks Cinnamon. The two girls make their way through the apartment to Cinnamon's en-suite bathroom.

"I don't know, girl. I feel weird. I'm scared as hell… my period has never been more than a week late and now it's *two*…" Cinnamon replies. "And I didn't even tell Zeke that I was late yet," Cinnamon adds before tears start falling from her eyes.

"Everything will be fine. Once you know the test results, we can come up with a plan," Mercedes says as she moves in to hug and comfort Cinnamon.

"...Okay, you're right. There's no point in stressing before I even know the results of the test... and I can't wait anymore; I need to know now," Cinnamon says.

"Ill be right here with you... the whole time."

"Ugh, I know Zeke's probably going to be so mad, but I'm going to text him right now."

Max is driving his black SUV; Zeke sits in the rear passenger's seat behind his grandmother.

"The second brown one on the right," Zeke points out to Max from the back seat. Zeke rushes out the back of the car, and then he returns to give his grandmother a kiss on the cheek and his brother a dap.

"Respects, bro; I'll let you know what's going on," Zeke says to Max while turning around to head inside the building to Cinnamon's apartment.

Zeke waits anxiously at the front door for Cinnamon to buzz him in.

Just as Zeke approaches Cinnamon's apartment, he can hear Cinnamon's voice talking with another female voice.

"I don't know what I'm going to do, girl. Street dudes don't just be having babies. I can't do this on my own."

"It'll be okay. Don't worry; just say how you feel. I'm sure he'll understand."

"Okay, okay, you're right. Well, I buzzed him in. He'll be here any minute."

As Zeke is finally about to knock on the door, it opens.

Mercedes walks out the door at the same time Zeke comes in.

"Ill catch you later, Cinny; text me," Mercedes says to Cinnamon before walking to the elevator.

Zeke notices the aura around his girl; he can feel it in his gut that things are getting serious.

"Come in, baby," Cinnamon says to Zeke; with a slight tremor in her hands, she attempts to slowly close the door behind him.

Stunned, Zeke notices an empty drugstore bag on the island in the kitchen, and all of a sudden, it seems that everything he is suspecting is falling in line one-by-one.

Even though the apartment is empty, Cinnamon leads Zeke to her room to have a more private conversation.

Cinnamon, sitting down on her perfectly made bed, hand gestures Zeke to have a seat next to her.

"You know I'm the type of girl to just say how it is, but I really don't even know how to say this," Cinnamon says to Zeke. She avoids making direct eye contact with him.

"You know you can tell me anything, baby... You know I love you and I'm here for you no matter what," Zeke says to Cinnamon to comfort her, as he can see she's on the brink of crying.

Cinnamon sniffles, "Zeke, I missed my period... like missed, missed it."

"Yea, I saw the bag in the kitchen... did you take the test already?" Zeke asks Cinnamon so he can see the results with his own eyes and not just with a gut feeling.

"Yuh... Yeah, it's on the counter in the bathroom." Scared for what might come next, Cinnamon doesn't follow Zeke into the bathroom; she already knows the results of the test.

"CINNAMON!! You're pregnant for reallll!!" Zeke yells with excitement from the bathroom to Cinnamon.

Confused at the tone, she stands up and joins Zeke in the washroom. Pinching her eyebrows, she says, "I'm pregnant, Zeke," in case he doesn't fully understand.

"So, what have you decided to do about it?" Zeke replies.

"Look, Zeke... I know we never really gave thought about having kids at this age, but I don't think I could ever forgive myself if I had an abortion. I would always think about him or her in the future and I just wouldn't be able to live with myself," Cinnamon explains her side to Zeke.

"Listen... I would never make you go through that. I know we haven't given it much thought but... that's our situation now, and to be honest, I don't think I could be happier," Zeke says to Cinnamon with a gigantic smile on his face.

"Really! Oh my goodness, that makes me so happy to hear, but you can't be a father and in the streets at the same time, though," Cinnamon professes.

"Don't worry about that, babygirl; I got it. I don't plan to stay in the streets forever, but it's gonna take time. You can't just jump back on the porch like that," Zeke says to Cinnamon. "But I plan to take back that construction job I did when I was younger. I can make good money there," Zeke assures Cinnamon so that she will feel at ease during the pregnancy.

Grama -	68	Miriam Fitzner
Fit -	23	Zeke Fitzner
Max -	19	Max Fitzner
Cinnamon -	23	Cinnamon Lockheart
Mercedes -	22	Mercedes Hawkin

Chapter 8

Everyone here?

April 2020

All phones vibrate with a video message

It's the groupchat. Von opens the chat because he sees it's from Jameel. "Finally. I been wondering where this guy was..." Von says out loud to Max, Dre, and Fit.

Like a fast-approaching thunderstorm, the mood changes drastically. They watch the video. "HAHAH look at this fucking goof, you guys aren't sick don't get caught lacking like this HAHAHAH... yo if you want your boy back bring 20 bands to the address" the opps say in the video followed by an address and time to meet.

It's apparent some old enemies thought they had unfinished business. They had used Jams' face ID to access his phone to send a message to their groupchat.

Their initial reaction is quick. Max yells, "FUCK THAT; THIS THE ONLY NICKEL THEY GETTING FROM ME" while loading the last two rounds in his .357. Then, he flicks his wrist clockwise to close the loading tray. He knows that time is of the essence, and he also hasn't caught a body since his first two... So he is ecstatic.

The four come out the house armed as if on their last mission ever. They have all the guns and all the ammunition they could muster up on the spot: two assault rifles with two circle magazines that contain 60 rounds, three pistols with a blue-beam attachment, and a heavy pistol with an extended clip to hold 16 rounds. Max wouldn't dare leave his house without his favourite .357.

In the black SUV, Max is driving with a menacing smirk on his face and the .357 fully loaded on his lap. Beside him is Von in the passenger's seat clutching one of the pistols with the blue beam and the heavy pistol but holding them low enough so as to not be visible to anyone passing by. Fit is behind him with one of the ARs in his lap, circle clip hanging out. Fit pulls out his phone and sees a text from Cinnamon asking if he's still coming to the doctor's appointment with her later today for the first ultrasound for their baby, but he locks his phone. Dre has the other AR across both bended knees and the extra magazines by his feet on the ground under the driver's seat. All are singing along.

In the car playing Hundo MC – Killa Mentality

"Nah fuck all the disrespect someone gotta die
Revenge ain't shit less you get it fore' the blood dry"

Pulling up to the address after an hour-and-a-half drive out of the city, the guys only have one thing on their mind: kill anybody in the way of saving their friend, Jams.

They have arrived at a secluded place, a two-storey cabin in the woods. It looks a little rundown, with a small broken window at the front overlooking the porch. Large forest trees surround an open area.

Walking in a line, Max, Von, Fit, and Dre stop right in front of the cabin. Bringing the assault rifles to the ready position, they let off warning rounds out of both assault rifles into the air. Hearing yelling and screams, Max stares at everything around and examines his surroundings. He soon calculates that there are seven guys total at the cabin including Jams.

After the gunshots have ceased, Max notices someone looking out of the upstairs window. "DUCKK!" Max yells. The four split and strategically hide behind trees and rocks as cover. Soon, shots are being exchanged back and forth from the house and the woods. There are two opps left and they have Jams tied up by his hands and feet with a pillowcase over his head.

Jams is with a new girl, Nunu, from an enemy territory. Being where he's from sleeping with an enemys girlfriend gets extra ratings. They had just gone to the burger joint downtown and ordered a small chicken burger with a side of fries each. Leaving the restaurant through the front doors, on their way back to the car in the parking lot, Jams notices Nunu dropped her phone, but he doesn't wait for her to pick it up. He keeps walking a few feet until she catches up with him.

What he doesn't know is that she had purposely dropped her phone so that she could send a text: "the plan is in action."

Jams usually drops off Nunu a few minutes' walk from her place because the war that's going on now knows no bounds, his enemys wouldn't miss. An opportunity to get him even if he was on a date. But this time, Nunu asks Jameel to drive her all the way to her house because her shoes are uncomfortable. Contemplating this, Jams agrees to bring her to her home because he brought his gun with him.

"You strong, right? Ive been thinking about reorganizing my living room all day you think you can help me move my couch? It's too heavy for me," Nunu requests.

"Shieeet," he says while unlocking the driver's side door along with the passenger's. He knows he is bout to get some action.

Nunu's plan has worked even better than expected. All she has to do is keep him there until the guys get there. She enters first and holds the door for Jams to come in behind her. She then closes the door but leaves it unlocked.

"Where your room at?" Jams says without wasting any time.

"I said my couch, dude," Nunu responds, partially offended at his straightforward question.

"Whatever, this black one right here?" Jams laughs. Nunu brushes this off as she's trying to be friendly to ensure her plan works accordingly.

They both go over to the couch and begin to strip each other and kiss. Jams knows he's in rival territory, so he knows he can't stay too long. Since this was only his third meeting with Nunu; he reaches his hand into the left pocket of his grey sweatpants and finds a cherry flavoured condom and hands it to Nunu.

Nunu, who is doing her best to impress Jameel, uses her mouth to place the condom over Jameel's pulsating penis. She begins to swallow his gurth while keeping eye contact with Jameel. He is doing his best to keep his composure but, letting out a deep grunt. Eventually leaning his head over the back of the couch, eyes rolled back, he reaches forward and grabs Nunu's long puffy ponytail and forcing his growth to go even deeper down her throat.

Just when Nunu begins to gasp for air he pulls her head up. Saliva dripping down the side of her mouth and off her chin onto the couch "comere" He says. Jameel reaches and grabs Nunu's right arm and pulls her closer for a kiss. He moves both his hands on to her face as she adjusts her position to sitting directly on top of him. Moaning in her mouth turned her on even more.

Nunu couldn't resist anymore, rubbing herself she puts Jameel's penis inside for him. Feeling how tight Nunu was Jameel pulls on her ponytail to have full control over her body.

Jameel uses his big muscular arms to pick up a sweaty Nunu and places her over the couch and starts pounding away, slapping her ass and pulling her hair as she leaves scratch marks on the black leather couch.

Twelve minutes go by and he pulls out just before erupting all over her backside. "Holy fuck; that was amazing. Where did you learn all that?" exclaims Nunu. She did think the sex was great but she adds in a few extra compliments in an attempt to boost Jameel's spirits so he will stay awhile longer.

But he is always aware of his surroundings and plans to head out. "Aha, yea, yea, I'm just naturally gifted; what can I say?" Jams says while sticking one leg through the bottom of his grey sweat-suit. Out of ideas, Nunu runs to the door to block it and kiss Jams once more. Suspicious of this, he looks around and notices the door was never locked. "You bitch; you tried to set me up!" Jams yells. At that second he then tries to run past her to escape through the door, but it is already being kicked in. Six men run into the house with guns all pointed at Jams. "FUCKK!" Jams shouts.

He knows that this is not a position he can fight out of as he left his gun in the car. "You know you look like a scared little bitch right now," the first man says to Jams. Jams recognizes one of the guys to be the last person Max didn't shoot at the club a few nights ago.

"You mean the face your mom makes when I pull my dick ou..." Jams is talking shit but gets pistol-whipped and knocked out.

BACK IN THE WOODS

Max, Von, Dre, and Fitz all enter the house after the shootout. They begin to look through the bottom level in search for Jams or any survivors. "HELLOO? YEOO JAMS, WHERE YOU AT?" Von calls out. Jams tries moaning as loud as he can because his mouth has been duct-taped. The crew hears his ruckus coming from upstairs.

They head toward the staircase with weapons still drawn, just in case. Leading the line is Von, followed by Max, Fit, and then Dre. They notice that there are two rooms on the upstairs level: one on the left and one straight ahead in which they can see Jams.

Von sprints over to a bleeding and egregiously beaten Jams, but as he runs past the first door on the left, he is blindsided. A gunman has pistol-whipped Von unconscious. Dre raises his weapon in retaliation, then a shot airs out. Dre turns his head quickly to the side in shock to notice Max holding his .357 with gun smoke coming out of it.

"My dad taught me you could die in the time it takes to hesitate." Max says.

After a moment of no one moving, Fitz says, "Let's get Jams and Von and get out of here." After untying Jams and picking up Von, they hear dogs barking and chains dangling. Since Fitz is closest to the window, he looks outside. "FUCK, that scared me. It's just someone jogging with their dogs," he yells out.

Max -	19	Max Fitzner
Fit -	23	Zeke Fitzner
Nunu -	19	Nuisha Jenkins
Jams -	19	Jameel Magou
Von -	23	Von Lampton
Dre -	34	Andre Lampton

Chapter 9

Quite the Encounter

December 1995

Santos and his loyal gang-banging friends, Rufus and John, decide to go to the roller skating place in Mississauga. Santos approaches the front doors of the roller rink and the two friends walk hurriedly ahead to open the doors before he gets there. He responds with a head nod, looking straight ahead without interrupting his step.

The three men walk to the counter to order inline skates. "Lemme get the best size 12s you got," Santos says.

"Sorry, we're out of size 12. Would you prefer 13 or 11?" the clerk asks. Santos cringes his eyes and balls his fist while resting his arm on the counter but doesn't say anything.

Seeing this, Rufus' eyes widen. "Listen, my girl, the boss said size 12," he restates sternly.

"Well, where would you like me to get them from then?" the clerk responds with a lot of attitude. John hears this as he returns to the counter with inline skates. He plops them on the counter in front of Santos.

"Here boss, 12s," says John.

"Where you find these?"

Santos turns to face John and looks him in the eyes and chuckles.

"Took em off that guy over there," John points to where he left the man barefooted.

Santos starts walking to a lane without paying for anything. The two friends follow after getting their own shoes.

Following behind Santos in a triangle formation, they noticed the boss stop suddenly. "Woah..." Santos utters before the guys can even ask the question. They're looking at the back of the boss then toward each other, their body language asking what is he talking about? They look at where the boss is facing and notice a birthday party going on in a corner of the rink. They see silver and gold banners hanging down with "Happy 18th birthday Nessa" written on them in a section just closed off to them.

Santos has laid his eyes on the most beautiful woman he has ever seen. Heading straight towards her and her group of friends who are conversing, he is on a mission to make her his. Santos has been with multiple women in the past, but this time is different. Even at his tender age of 19, he knows there will never be a better catch than her.

"Hey, babygirl, lemme holla at you," Santos says in the middle of the group, interrupting their conversation. She has been watching Santos since the moment his friends opened the door for him without him saying anything.

Visibly blushing hard, she grabs her pearls around her neck and walks through the middle of the group to follow him.

Rufus and John create a barrier, standing side by side so that no one can walk up to the boss without him knowing.

Santos' heart is beating at what feels like 200 times a minute. "My name is James," Santos says. Shocked that he is so nervous, he says his government name instead of Santos. He grabs the brim of his fitted hat and pulls it down, rolling his eyes at his mistake.

She giggles and places a hand on his chest softly and responds, "My name is Vanessa, but everyone just calls me Nessa."

Her hand on his chest makes him feel even more off balance. "So, it's your birthday, uh?" James says while attempting to clear his throat. She loves that she can make a gangster weak for her, but she has no idea to what extent James is involved in the street life.

What seems like 45 minutes has passed, and the boss returns, walking between John and Rufus followed by Vanessa. James is guiding her by the hand.

James drops her back off with her friends, whispers something to her, gives her a hug, and sends her away.

"We out," Santos says to John and Rufus while raising his hand and signalling the door.

The next day, at around 6:30 p.m., James uses the number on the piece of paper Vanessa had given to him the previous day to call her house phone.

"Hello," Vanessa answers swiftly.

February 1996

Vanessa is ready to let James meet her father, Kris, over dinner at her house on Thursday night. She has been skeptical of this because she knows her father is also a man who works in the streets of Toronto, but her love for James has grown past the nervousness of the meeting.

James knocks on the door. Vanessa sprints downstairs in her brand-new jeans outfit and styling finger waves. Placing her hand on the doorknob and looking through the peephole, she takes a deep breath to calm herself down. "Who issss it?" Vanessa sings through the closed door.

"Gaddamn mama I can see how fine you are through the door." He can't, but James is a pleaser.

She opens the door and wraps both arms around his neck, nearly jumping into his arms. He steps inside and takes off his shoes to see a man walking in the kitchen carrying plates. "Daddy, he's here!" Vanessa shouts without taking her eyes off of James. She is smiling from her soul.

Her father walks down the hallway toward the door. All Vanessa's father can see at this point is a teenage boy bent over, taking off his shoes. The second James stands up, Vanessa's father's eyes pop open at the sight. A moment of silence passes.

"This is your father, baby?" James says while staring at Kris.

"You know my father? James?" she questions, very confused.

Her father cuts her off. "S...Santos?? What are you doing here; I don't pick up from you until this weekend," Kris says in an unusually soft and apologetic voice never heard before to Vanessa while slowly raising his arms, bent at the elbow as if to surrender.

"Kay K, you strapped?" James asks.

"Ye-yeah, why?" Kris says hesitantly.

Reaching out his arm, Santos waits for the gun to be placed in his hand. Kris reaches in his back waistband and places a .357 with a customized white handle with gold engravings in James' hands. James tucks it in his back waistband, and then he proceeds to the kitchen.

Vanessa -	18	Vanessa Kyle
Santos -	19	James Fitzner
Rufus -	22	Robert Manson
John -	21	Johnathan Cobain
Kay K -	39	Kris Kyle

Chapter 10

At the Hospital

December 2020

Rushing inside the hospital for a wheelchair, Zeke slams his right shoulder into the automatic door before it fully opens. Stumbling through the entrance, he fortunately finds an unoccupied wheelchair. Back at the car is Max helping an in-labour Cinnamon stand up while they wait for the wheelchair to arrive. As Zeke arrives with the wheelchair, he sees Cinnamon in obvious discomfort and labour pains. Zeke takes over from Max and helps Cinnamon into the wheelchair and starts to wheel toward the entrance once again.

This time slightly more calmly, Zeke enters the hospital and stops the first hospital worker that he sees. It happens to be an old man with a white power donut hairstyle sporting dark blue scrubs.

"Hey YO, can you help me? My girlfriend's water broke about 20 minutes ago; she is having our baby," Zeke says, panicking to the doctor.

"Right this way, sir." Dr. Mohammed leads them to an empty room while he prepares his staff to deliver the baby.

Zeke crouches down to sit on his ankles. "Everything is gonna be fine, Cinny; we'll get through this as a team," he says as he reaches over and holds her hand. At this point, Cinnamon is in so much pain she can't even utter words in response so she just nods her head in agreement.

Zeke has never seen Cinnamon in so much pain in his life, and it is due to her pregnancy. Cinnamon isn't a soft girl by any means, as he knows firsthand by their play fights, so to see her cry from overbearing pain is a sight that is painful for him to watch.

Once they enter the room, Zeke helps Cinnamon change into the more comfortable gown that the doctor has laid out.

"Damn, how fat do they think I am? This thing is huge," Cinnamon says to Zeke as she holds up the sky-blue gown with dark blue polka dots.

"Rela... Chi... It's not that serious, baby... ahaha... I'm sure it's just one-size-fits-all, and they aren't actually measuring you; they're for everybody," Zeke says while chuckling at Cinnamon.

"...Whatever, gimme it."

"Man, I'm going to be a dad!!! I hope he plays sports; he could be Athlete of the year or something or better! Maybe football; with some practice he could be the greatest football player of all time. I hope he makes lots of friends and no one takes advantage of him, but of course I'll be teaching him that from today," Zeke is ranting about his future plans for his child.

Cinnamon is just so mesmerized by Zeke talking about their future together that she doesn't say anything; she just lets him continue going on...

"I see the crown, Ms. Lockheart. You're doing really well, but I'm going to need you to push harder," Dr. Mohammed says to Cinnamon.

"You got this, babe; just a little bit more," Zeke says while holding her hand at the bedside.

With Max and the nurses cheering her on so adamantly, Cinnamon yells, "If y'all ain't gon switch up and do this for me, shut the fuck UP!"

Max scratches his head, feeling awkward and out of place; he silently tells Zeke he's gonna get everyone something to drink so he can slip out.

After 77 minutes of hard labour, a baby is born to Zeke Fitzner and Cinnamon Lockheart. There is a moment of silence, and then a new cry fills the room. Dr. Mohammed places the newborn baby on Cinnamon's chest. She begins to cry because she is absolutely stunned. She had no idea it was possible for a human to love something too much. She kisses the baby on the cheek. "We'll call her Violet."

Zeke loves the name. "Violet it is! Mannn, this is my baby girl! Violet Fitzner..." Zeke is ecstatic.

Dr. Mohammed pauses right before standing up to take off his gloves. "...Did you two know you're having babies?" he says to both of them huddling over Violet.

"We're having baBIES??" Zeke's eyes pop open at the news.

Cinnamon opens her eyes and says, "Reallyy? Are you sure?" She knew it was a possibility for her to have twins as it runs in her family. And after Zeke missed their first two ultrasound appointments, she never set another one.

"This is insane!! WE'RE HAVING ANOTHER ONE!" Zeke shouts out in excitement. A nurse brings Violet to the delivery area where newborn babies are examined and the rest of the nurses start preparing for the next delivery.

"I see the crown on this one protruding, Ms. Lockheart. I'm going to ask you for one last push and we can do the rest."

"Okay, he's out," Dr. Mohammed says.

"HEEE??!! YESS!" Zeke screams out.

But the doctor's expression changes quite drastically.

The newborn baby isn't breathing.

"Nurse Reece, go open up lab B ASAP," Dr. Mohammed says. Nurse Reece runs out the room.

Zeke and Cinnamon are both lost in confusion. "WHAT is going on Doc?? What do you mean he isn't breathing!!" says Zeke.

"His breathing is very weak and irregular, and I'm going to do my best to figure out the problem as quickly as I can so that we can save your child," Dr. Mohammed explains to the parents.

The nurses take the newborn baby in a customized baby stretcher to a location where they can do the necessary work. Zeke assures Cinnamon that everything will be okay and explains that she should rest. He will take care of it.

Running down the hallway to catch up with the speeding nurse, he passes an intersection. At the end of the hallway perpendicular to him is Max, being escorted out of the hospital in handcuffs by two police officers.

"FUCK FUCK FUCK what am I supposed to do?" Zeke is contemplating to himself.

He arrives at the doors just after the nurses enter with his son.

Max -	19	Max Fitzner
Fit -	23	Zeke Fitzner
Cinnamon -	23	Cinnamon Lockheart
Violet -	0	Violet Fitzner

Baby #2 - ???

Chapter 11

Locked?

December 2020

"Yo, Jams, come play cards," Max says to Jams in general population. Jams sits on the bench with Max. "Don't worry, my dude, they don't got nothing on us that puts us at rebellion. We straight."

"Yee, we'll be on roads again before you know it," Jams replies to Max.

"Yo, that nigga right there been looking at me since yesterday when we got in here," Max says while dealing cards.

"Which nigga wanna die up in this bitch," Jams replies to Max.

"Aye, you might not wanna fuck with Rufus; he's very high-ranking in here," a stranger says.

"We gon find out right now; here he comes," Max says.

Jams stands up, ready for whatever as the man approaches the bench.

"Jheez, you look just like him," Rufus says to Max.

"Huh? Like who?" Max replies.

"You a Fitzner, no? I used to run with your Pops back in the day." Jams sits down.

"You knew my pops?" Max says.

"Yea, that war cost us a lot. I'm sorry about your father, Santos," Rufus says.

"Respects... So, you know who killed my father?" Max has always wanted to know.

"Yea, some nigga named Rizzo Lampton... I got the drop on him a few weeks after they got your father and I sprayed up his block." Max respected him for retaliating in honour of his father.

"Ah, so you got him then?"

"It just so happened I only hit him and ended up killing the guys with him, but he's paralyzed from the waist down so it is what it is."

Max grinds his teeth. "That's not enough." Max wants him dead from taking his father away from him. He figures he needs him to pay even more.

"Wait, you said Lampton...? Ain't that Dre and Von's peoples?" Jams says to them both. Max pauses to think and looks at Rufus.

"Well, I only know he had one kid in Niagara... Andre."

"Not two? Andre and Von are brothers."

"Or they could just be cousins and they lying to save themselves."

"You right... Dre gotta pay for this. He been holding out this whole time."

Banging from the cell opening

"Mr. Fitzner, you have a visitor."

"Hey baby, I miss you," Ashley says to Max.

"I miss you too," Max says to Ashley. But Ashley can tell something is weighing heavily on Max's mind.

"What's going on, Max? Talk to me. You don't look so good; you've lost a lot of weight," Ashley says, concerned that the case against Max may be getting worse.

"I just found out who killed my father..." Ashley is stunned. She has never seen Max with such seriousness in his face since the night at Rebellion.

"Wow, I'm so sorry about that, but that's just another reason I need you to be out here with me."

"Thank you, babygirl, but I don't know how imma get out of this one. They got me and Jams in here for it."

"Well, you're always saying how Jams owes you. Tell him to take this one since he has a clean record," Ashley says to Max. Max is interested in this idea. He contemplates it. Inside, Max is burning with rage that he has to get revenge on Andre for his father. If this is his only way to make it happen, he has to at least give it a try.

"You're right; he owes me. I got shit to take care of. If he's really my guy, he should get that."

"Yo Jams, lemme holla at you," Max says to Jameel.

"What's good witchu, M?" Jams responds.

"I gotta ask you a favour, my nigga; real shit," Max says to Jams.

"What poppin?"

"I know you remember bout that shit Uncle Rufus said about my pops and Dre..."

"Yea that shit is foul. That nigga Dre needs to answer some questions."

"Yea, and that's exactly what I'm saying... Can you do me a favour and take this charge so I can smoke that nigga Rizzo for my pops?" Max says to Jams, unsure of what his reaction will be.

Jams is stunned at this. He's speechless.

"Yo, I'll hold down anything and everything you need on the outside, my G, but this shit is personal," Max adds since Jams hasn't responded.

"You know what, yo... I knew you were never built for this jail life... I better not see your ass back in here, uh."

"My G, you don't know what this means to me... No nigga can ever talk bad about you around me."

"I'll call my lawyer tomorrow," Jams responds to Max.

Max -	19		Max Fitzner
Jams -	19		Jameel Magou
Ashley -	21		Ashley Gibson
Rufus -	57		Robert Manson

Chapter 12

Brotherly One-on-One

December 2020

Knocking on the door

"That has to be him!" Zeke hops up and hands Violet to Cinnamon as he rushes to the door. Looking through the peephole, all he needs to see is that big blob of hair and he knows exactly who it is.

"Welcome home, Max!!" says Zeke as he nearly pulls the handle out of the door. It has been two weeks since he saw him being escorted out of the hospital on the day Violet was born.

"Yooo, how you been, fam?" Max asks Zeke as he wraps his arms tightly around his brother.

"Hello, Zeke; hello, Cinnamon; see, it didn't take me that long to get here," says Ashley, holding her purse and Max's bag of items from Toronto South.

"Hey girl, and welcome home, Max; we've missed you here," Cinnamon says to Max and Ashley.

"Aweee, is this my little niece Violet?" he says as he walks over to Cinnamon. Cinnamon hands Violet to Max, and he rocks her in his arms and makes faces.

"You guys are just in time. I am making some rice and peas and oxtail; it'll be ready in five minutes," Cinnamon says.

"Yo, Zeke, we gotta talk after," Max says to Zeke in a serious tone.

Man, I'm so sorry about the death of your second child, and even more mad at myself for missing the funeral," Max states.

"Yea man, we're trying to take it day-by-day to move forward, but some days are easier than others," Zeke responds. After a pause, Zeke asks, "So, yo Jams really did that for you, eh?"

"Yea, he's really taking the L for me; he saved my life."

"That shit is crazy. I can't thank him enough for that; real nigga, for real."

"But he didn't just do that for no reason... When in there, we met a solid nigga named Rufus. He used to run with Dad back in the day."

"What? He used to run with DAD??"

"Yea, but that's not all. The man who killed Dad is... Andre's father, *Rizzo Lampton*."

"Say swear to God..." Zeke says to Max, but Max just stares into Zeke's eyes and remains silent. Zeke is shocked in disbelief.

"Goddamn that nigga Dre for real... and he ain't said shit this whole time and neither did Von. We can't let that shit slide."

"Exactly... I'm glad you said that. While I was inside, this is what I came up with," Max says to Zeke.

Ashley -	20		Ashley Gibson
Max -	19		Max Fitzner
Fit -	23		Zeke Fitzner
Violet -	0		Violet Fitzner
Cinnamon -	23		Cinnamon Lockheart

Chapter 13

On a Mission

Christmas Eve Eve 2020

"You ready, Zeke? We leaving in five minutes," Max says while tucking his .357 in his black bubble jacket pocket.

"As ready as I can be for this," Zeke responds.

"Look yo, if you want, I can just go inside and you drive; you don't need to come in." Max knows Zeke inside and out. It isn't the fact that they are going to hurt someone; it is the fact that it is someone so close to him that he is about to do it to.

"Nah, Dre gotta pay for what he's done." Max could see straight through Zeke's words.

"We're just going to get him to tell us where his father is, right?"

"Yea, then we take his ass out."

"Take who out?"

"Rizzo, Man"

"Yuh... Yeah, I can deal with that; let's go," Zeke responds to Max with fire in his eyes.

"I told him we're coming for some drinks since I'm fresh out of jail, so he won't suspect a thing."

As the two head out and start driving toward Andre's house, Max starts playing some music to help ease Zeke's mind on the situation.

"C'mon, b, turn it down; this is serious."

"Sheesh, fam, you're never like this. Wassup? You good?" Max asks.

"My bad, yo. I don't mean to come off like that, but this parenting shit's hard. I haven't slept in a day and a half," Zeke explains to Max. Thinking about his brother's situation and their family, Max is leaning more and more toward not letting his brother come inside on the mission.

"We're here," Zeke says as he arrives in Andre's neighbourhood. Zeke parks on the right side of the road, a few spots down from Andre's house.

"I got this, yo. Don't worry; I'll talk to him," Max says to Zeke as he exits the car.

Knocks on the door

"Ayeee, Max, whatchu sayin? And where Zeke at?" Andre opens the front door with greetings. Max remains silent but grinds his teeth at the sight of Andre. Filled with hatred and rage, he can't even utter words.

"Yo, what's goin' on, fam?" Andre says as he takes a step back to assess the situation, but it's too late. Max gives Andre an uppercut that leaves him seeing stars.

"I had your life in my hands. I should've aimed for you in that cabin in the woods," Max shouts at Andre as he is mounting him.

Still dazed, Andre says, "What are you talking about, yo?" while spitting out blood from his mouth.

"Listen… I came here to hurt you for as long as it takes for you to tell me where your father or uncle or whatever *Rizzo* is," Max says before giving Andre two powerful strikes to his nose.

"I could never do that, knowing what you plan to do to him… 'Cause I would never do that to you," Andre replies to Max.

Max knows that what Andre is saying isn't a lie, he would never give up someone that was close to him, but Max doesn't lose all hope. He knows that if Andre isn't going to give him the info he needs, he will take out his anger on the person closest to Rizzo.

Fit - 23	Zeke Fitzner
Max - 19	Max Fitzner
Dre - 34	Andre Lampton

Chapter 14

May 200X

Santos and Vanessa are living together in a beautiful two-storey home in the heart of Toronto. Anticipating having three children, Santos sees the four-bedroom house as a golden opportunity.

The house is at the back of a cul-de-sac, perfect for protecting his house and taking his business to the next level. Santos at 21 has fully paid off this $700,000 house in cash — with the money he had been cleaning through a chain of beauty supply stores— before moving in.

With Santos carrying the love of his life Vanessa over the threshold of their new house, they had both stopped and a taken a breath as if that would set in their heads that they have their own place.

The first floor features a den immediately to their left, followed by u-shaped staircases leading upstairs and to the basement. Down the hallway is the dining room followed by the kitchen. This is where James and Vanessa spend most of their time when James isn't running his business, as they both love to cook together.

Earlier in the day, James had caught a scent of new competition sprouting up. This is nothing new to James, as there are always people trying to make a name for themselves in the drug game, but just as a precautionary measure, James sets up a meeting to pick up from the rival to see if the product itself is something to worry about. James has set up a pickup with the kingpin from Niagara, Rizzo, for 5 p.m.

James is far more intelligent than the average 21-year-old in terms of street smarts. Appearing at the first meeting with an untrustworthy source is out of the question. James sends Marcus and

Kay K, who are two ranks below John and Rufus in his organization.

Rizzo is well known across the Greater Toronto Area for having the purest cocaine. Being in Niagara is perfect for Rizzo because he can get his shipments right off the boat and not be forced to have a chain of command. For Rizzo, being his own boss is his number one aspiration and what guides him to the top of the game.

James' phone rings; it's John. Before he answers, he looks at Vanessa with loving eyes and says, "Gimme a second, Ness." He walks a few steps into the living room, wiping flour residue off on his apron.

"Hey boss, we gotta problem," John says. James sighs and hangs up immediately. He knows exactly what the problem is and has anticipated a solution for quick resolve. It is his first pickup from a kingpin from Niagara, so he doesn't know what to expect. This is a rival of James who now borders his territory.

Santos brings a fiend along to meet with Kay K and Marcus.

"Where is it?" Santos demands.

Kay K hands over the package of what was supposed to be one kilo of pure cocaine. Santos retrieves his rusty switchblade that is tucked in the breast pocket of his jacket and cuts the package open. "Here!" He holds the coke up for the fiend. The fiend, mouth salivating, almost can't wait for the signal and stuffs half of his nose in the product. Seeing this, Santos instantly knows he has to get this connect. Santos has made it this far with average product, and so with a top of the line product, he believes he can take over the world. Santos looks at Marcus and Kay K and says, "I'll let you know when's the next meeting."

Santos has been building a rapport with Rizzo but with the idea to get close enough to take his business from right under him. But Rizzo, being much older and more experienced in the game, would never let anyone he didn't know since before he started in the game get close to him — some would call it trust issues, but for good reason.

Santos and Rizzo aren't friends by any means, but they have an underlying respect for one another. Neither can see weak points in each other's empire.

Some years later, Santos has found out Rizzo's shipment times and locations through a snitch. Santos' plan is to rob a shipment sent to Rizzo so that he will become untrustworthy and he could be the main connect. But Rizzo, having eyes and ears in Toronto as well, issues a public statement. "Santos, if you try anything, we are going to war, no if, ands, or buts." Hearing this, Santos is momentarily hesitant, but he knows that the two can't compete forever.

Santos gets the ship robbed just as he planned and a war follows shortly after. Rizzo is at an advantage because he had lived in Toronto briefly during his teenage years. Aside from having connections in the city, he knows the geographical landscape of Toronto and is easily able to find out the location of any picture Vanessa or Santos posts online.

At the height of the war when Santos has already sent the majority of his shooters to Niagara to end Rizzo once and for all, considering the tense situation he has Vanessa out of town to show face for a grand opening of their own beauty salon so that she won't be in harm's way. He figures his sons will be safe in his personal care because he knows no one would watch out for them like he would.

Santos and his two sons Zeke and Max are on their way home from Zeke's first basketball game. "Hey Zee, when you learn all them dribble moves, those kids can't do anything to stop you," Santos states enthusiastically.

"Haha, man, this must how Kobe feels; it's too easy," Zeke says, laughing with his father. "Nahh, I'm pretty sure Kobe don't even make it look that easy. As a treat, where y'all wanna eat?" Santos asks both of his sons.

"Burgers!" they shout.

Inside, Santos orders three kids' meals for himself and his sons. Santos has made it an objective to eat the same thing as his sons because he feels like that will make his sons feel equal to him. Carrying the three trays at once, they find a booth to sit in. Santos lets his sons choose where they want to sit. Luckily for him, he gets to have his back to the wall where he feels most comfortable. He talks to his sons about the great debate between three legendary basketball players.

Shortly after bringing his sons to the washroom to wash their hands, they get back to the car and head home.

As it is a school night for Zeke — Max hasn't started school yet — he tucks him into bed. James asks if Max wants to watch a movie with him as he is in high spirits due to Zeke's basketball performance. Santos turns off the light, wishing Zeke sweet dreams. He gives him a kiss on his forehead before carrying Max in his one arm to the living room.

"What you wanna watch, big guy?" James asks, almost placing his face on Max's.

"*Detective Kids*!" Max yells, raising his arms in excitement.

"Ok, buddy, give me a sec." James remembers he hasn't changed the batteries for the remote and the last time they were dead. Once he returns, Max complains to him it's too hot so he cracks open the kitchen window.

After the movie finishes, he puts Max to bed, goes into his lonely room, and turns on the light…

Rizzo has been stalking Santos since before the basketball game. Staring at the house, awaiting a God-given sign, he sees Santos' room light turn on. "Perfect," he says, pulling down his ski mask with a menacing smirk. Rizzo reaches over to grab the fully loaded riot shotgun with the drum attachment. "This guy wants to play? I'll show him how a *real nigga* plays," Rizzo whispers to himself. Shutting his black SUV door quietly, he makes his way to the house.

Rizzo does a full round of the house to get familiar with the layout, and he notices the kitchen window slightly open. Seeing this, Rizzo thinks this is too easy. At first, Rizzo was very confident in his abilities to remain incognito; however, seeing a window open at a top drug lord's house the night he plans to do a home invasion makes him very skeptical — but it's too late to turn back— so he proceeds with extra caution. Tip-toeing through the kitchen and then up the stairs, he hears the shower running. Passing a closed door where he figures Santos' kids are sleeping — Rizzo has no beef with kids as he has one of his own — he goes to Santos' room.

The entire house is dead silent. Rizzo lifts his right heel in front of him and gives the door a powerful kick, nearly breaking it off the hinges. "Santos, GET OUT HERE; I TOLD YOU THIS WOULD FUCKING HAPPEN!" Rizzo yells through the semi-closed door. Not hearing anything, he uses the barrel of the riot shotgun to slowly push the door fully open.

Through the door hinges he can see Santos, naked and trying to hide behind the door. "Get out here," he repeats. Santos remains silent, biting his teeth, but he follows his command.

"You hear that, Zee?" Max questions with extreme anxiety. But his brother doesn't wake up. Scared for his life, Max has a gut feeling something is wrong and it isn't just another movie he is hearing from their room. Leaving his bed, he crawls to the door on hands and knees to be as quiet as possible. Max opens the door slowly so that he can investigate without being seen. To Max's surprise, he sees a man standing over his naked father with a big gun in his hand that reads "*Rizzo*" in cursive engraved into it.

He can hear the mumbling of his father and the man conversing, but he can't make out any of what they are saying. Shocked at the never-before-experienced scene of danger, Max is paralyzed with fear.

Bang

Max -	3	Max Fitzner
Zeke -	6	Zeke Fitzner
Vanessa -	27	Vanessa Kyle
Santos -	28	James Fitzner
Rufus -	31	Robert Manson
John -	30	Johnathan Cobain
Kay K -	48	Kris Kyle

Chapter 15

Christmas Eve Eve 2020

This time, Max isn't paralyzed with fear.

Max raises his right hand as if pledging allegiance with the .357 in his hand and slams it down with all his might into the dead centre of Andre's face... again... and again until he feels the hardwood floor through the skull of Andre.

Quickly wiping the splattered blood from his face with the sleeve of his jacket; Max lightly jogs back to the car where Zeke has been waiting almost ten minutes. As soon as Max gets into the car, Zeke starts driving away.

"Yo, what happened? He told you where Rizzo at?" Zeke asks Max anxiously.

"I smoked him," Max answers Zeke.

Zeke's heart falls. "What the fuck? That wasn't the plan, yo. Fuck you mean you smoked him?"

"He wouldn't talk and I couldn't just leave him after doing him like that, he said he is going to warn Rizzo," Max defends himself.

"Nah bro, you could've avoided that," Zeke says angrily.

"You know what? I didn't want to… You have to learn what happens when you cross one of us."

"You got to think this shit through. You just got out and you caught another body," Zeke says to try to talk some sense into Max.

"And I'm not going back no matter what… you know what? I'll just walk from here. Let me out," Max cuts him off while talking.

"Aight. I know I shouldn't have to tell you this, but it's hot. Lay low for a bit," Zeke says as he lets Max out of the car.

Fit - 23   Zeke Fitzner
Max - 19   Max Fitzner
Dre - 34   Andre Lampton

Chapter 16

A surprise Visit?

December 2020

Text Message

Max: Yeo fam Jams called me yesterday and told me someone inside there is gonna rat on me for the Dre body, I don't know how someone would've known that but, FUCK!

I definitely can't go back.

Zeke: That's fucked bro you just got back out yo.

Max: I know I might actually go link that ting from Middle Tennessee and stay there permanently.

Max: Feds looking for me non stop... Last time I went near my place there were two police cars waiting on the block.

Zeke: Anything is better than going back to inside, but you really trust a girl from the States?

Max: Yaya the same one who stayed with me two years ago from Caribana plus I'm just going to tell her I need a new job, she's not gonna know why.

Knocking on Zeke's apartment door

"Hold up. Here, baby, hold her; let me get the door," Zeke says as he hands his daughter Violet to Cinnamon and leaves the bedroom. Sliding his feet into his slippers, he makes his way to the front door to check the peephole.

"What the fuck, the cops are here... If it was a raid, they wouldn't have knocked. They would've just busted in here," Zeke thinks to himself while looking at two men in police officer uniforms.

Without opening the door, Zeke asks, "Who are you looking for, officers?" in hopes that this is some sort of error and they came to the wrong place.

"We just have a few questions for... *Zeke Fitzner.*"

"*Fuck*" under his breath.

Zeke opens the door to speak to the police officers. "What do y'all want?" Zeke says to the officers before they have the chance to say anything.

"Hello, Zeke Fitzner, we would like you to come in for questioning."

"What's this regarding?" Zeke demands the officers.

"We're investigating the murder of Andre Lampton on Thursday of last week."

Zeke pauses to think before saying, "What? My best friend Andre is dead? How did this happen?"

"He was brutally beaten in his home is all the information I can give out, but if it's no problem with you, we'd like you to visit our office to clear your name in the case."

"Clear my name? Why would my name be in the case at all... I was with my grandmother at bingo night at the bingo house on Thursday."

"Your vehicle was seen in the area at the time of the murder. Mr. Fitzner, we can speak further about the subject in a more *private location*," the cop says. Before they leave, he hands Zeke a card with a phone number and address on it.

"What the fuck am I going to do, Cinnamon? They got my car in the area. I don't know how I can beat that," Zeke says, nearly in tears. Zeke's one wish is that his daughter won't grow up fatherless in this world where that has become the normal.

"I can't sit to the side and watch you go to jail for something you didn't even do..." Cinnamon says to Zeke. "If Max said that Jams owed him that last one, then Max owes you this one; plus, didn't you tell me someone is already snitching on him? So, if he's already going down, why do you have to go down with him?" Cinnamon adds.

"It's different, though. They were already locked up."

"Yea, and that's how you're going to end up too... away from me... and away from Violet when we need you the most," Cinnamon says as tears flow endlessly from her eyes.

"He's my brother; I knew him before he even knew himself... I'm supposed to be his guardian, his protector, his keeper."

She leaves the room with Violet.

Fit -	23	Zeke Fitzner
Cinnamon -	23	Cinnamon Lockheart
Violet -	0	Violet Fitzner
Officer Andrews -	39	Gregory Andrews

Chapter 17

New Year's Eve 2020

Shaking while taking the keys out his ignition, Zeke feels like he has the weight of the world on his shoulders. He sits back in his seat, holding his head and thinking a million and one thoughts. It is as if the car is filled with water and he is drowning.

A loud sigh escapes Zeke's lungs. "There can't be any mistakes here," he whispers to himself as he reaches for the car door handle.

As Zeke is approaching the door, two gentlemen are walking out. They are arguing about something that Zeke can barely make out.

"I'm telling you, bro, you did the right thing; trust me," one guy says before turning the corner.

Zeke hears this and kisses his teeth as he heads into the police department. The front desk is behind a huge glass separating the officers from the public.

"Hello, I'm here to see Mr. Andrews," Zeke says to the officer at the front desk.

"Have a seat right behind you; he'll be with you shortly," Officer Thomas answers Zeke.

The chairs are dark blue padded foam; they are extremely nice chairs for public seating. This makes Zeke uncomfortable because he knows that police always try to butter you up before they take advantage of you. This short time alone doesn't make Zeke feel any calmer; his thoughts are still running rampant in his head. Luckily for him, the wait doesn't last that long.

"Mr. Fitzner, right this way." Gregory Andrews comes out of a door wearing bell bottom blue jeans and a peach plaid button-up to greet Zeke. Gregory, a middle aged man, is bald with a full greyish-black beard.

Zeke looks up at Mr. Andrews and releases another sigh. "I guess it's time," Zeke says under his breath. Getting up feels like trying to drag a car out of the ocean. As Zeke is walking with Mr. Andrews to his office, they walk side by side down two hallways.

"Did you find the parking alright?" Gregory asks Zeke as he places a hand on Zeke's back.

Usually this would be an issue for Zeke because he does not like when people touch him, but he allows it. "Yeah, but I didn't pay for that long and I'm not tryna get towed," Zeke responds.

"No worries. We can take care of the cost of parking for you today, on me," Greg says. Zeke knows what Greg's goal is and that he will not be distracted from the results he needs today.

"Hello, Zeke, to formally introduce myself my name is Gregory Andrews... you can call me Greg."

Zeke remains silent...

"We have a witness who can identify Max running out of Andre Lampton's house to a vehicle at the time of the murder," Greg says to Zeke.

Zeke has already known about the witness and he remains calm and silent. Zeke thinks that as long as there is no new evidence, his plan won't be thrown off.

"We also have your car in the area..." Gregory says.

Zeke is stunned... His face turns whiter than chalk. Having his car in the area was already the biggest thing weighing on his mind, and now he finally has to face it. Zeke starts to think back to all the streets he took to see if he can remember if any of the stop lights had a red-light camera that could identify his face.

"I lend my car out a lot; I'm not sure where it was that night." Zeke has practiced this answer a thousand times over, but when the time actually comes, he is shaky.

"The last time we spoke at your apartment, you said you were at a bingo night with your grandmother."

"Yea, that's correct."

"So, I took the time to go over to the bingo house and check your alibi, but it turns out only a Miriam Fitzner can place you there that night, no one else," Greg said.

Even more shocked, Zeke couldn't believe his alibi fell through. Zeke is lost for words...

"Listen, we know Max is guilty of this... You can either tell us exactly how this night went or we can just end it right here and charge you as an accomplice in the murder of Andre Lampton. Think about your family; you have a daughter now. Are you just going to throw away your family? Are you sure that if he gets away with this, he won't get himself hurt or killed by someone else? In a way, this is like protecting him."

"Wait... I didn't even want to go with him."

New Year's Eve 2020

"So it really worked?" Cinnamon says with extreme happiness.

"Yeah, I'm home free now," Zeke says while hugging Cinnamon and his daughter Violet.

Zeke's plan has worked out exactly as he had hoped. He acted as if he had no intention on giving up his brother to ensure 100% immunity.

He knew that his best chance to be free and watch over his daughter was to give up his brother.

Zeke was mentally in turmoil. It was not easy to snitch on his only brother, but it was an impossible choice that had to be made. Thinking about all the times that it has been Max taking things too far getting them caught up, maybe he won't end up dead if he was in jail.

To choose between his only brother and his only daughter was the single hardest decision Zeke has had to make yet, but the thought of someone else raising his daughter pushed him over the edge.

Text message

Max: Yo bro I'm coming back… Jams showed me Rufus was the rat… He *took care of him* before he could take the stand.

Max: I Guess that's why they say, 'don't shoot the messenger'… *Cause you're actually supposed to.*

See you soon

Officer Andrews -	39	Gregory Andrews
Officer Thomas -	29	Micheal Thomas
Fit -	23	Zeke Fitzner
Max -	19	Max Fitzner
Cinnamon -	23	Cinnamon Lockheart
Violet -	0	Violet Fitzner

9 780228 838883